Tour of Atlantis

Walter Foster

Published by The New Star Press, 2023.

This is a work of fiction. Similarities to real people, places, or events are entirely coincidental.

TOUR OF ATLANTIS

First edition. February 9, 2023.

Copyright © 2023 Walter Foster.

ISBN: 979-8215652244

Written by Walter Foster.

Also by Walter Foster

Tour of Atlantis
The House on the Edge of Homerville
Blackula the Vampire!
The Invisible Man
Blackenstein
Diamonds on Mars!
Fragments: Abort Martian Landing
Madam Black Soothsayer - Fortune Teller

to Johnathan

*"TOUR
of
ATLANTIS"
by
Walt Foster*

Chapter

O*ne*

July 18, 2022

He was often seen early on the large front porch of his modest wood frame home. He usually sat there from sun up untill late in the day and when he wasn't there people usually came by to check on him. Mr. Julies Hampton was wheelchair bound and was 106 years old, the oldest known citizen of the small Fulton County neighborhood just outside Atlanta, Georgia. He had all his facilities and people knew he could talk up a storm when he wanted to. But when he didn't want to say anything, folks knew he could be as mum as they came. On the front porch, his wheelchair, to him, made sense. When the sun got into his eyes late in the day he could back it up to be more in the shade. In the morning the sun was *behind* the house and his chair was fully in the shade so it made no difference where he sat.

A wooden fence was just in front of the house, a sidewalk and a two way street was just beyond that. The fence was just lowered enough so that he could see the traffic passing by. Sometimes people would honk at him from the street. He made sure he waved back to acknowledge every one of them.

Those were the routine of his days.

Mr. Julies, despite his age took pride in what was going on around him. He wanted to know if they was widening the road, or building a new supermarket. He took the evening paper of *The Atlanta Constitution* so that he could stay on top of things.

Billy Joe Dupree, a young black boy delivered the paper to him daily but instead of flinging it into the yard like the others on his route, he would climb off of his bicycle and give Mr. Julies his paper personally.

"Thank, you Billy Boy," Mr. Julies would say.

Occasionally, Billy would stop for a few moments of chat.

Then he'd be on his way.

Gloria Caldwell was Mr. Julies' neice. She was 47 years old

and not yet married. She had no suiters. To all who cared to notice,

it seemed her prime objective was to take care of her twice married,

twice widowed great uncle, Mr. Julies, and she did a masterful

job of that, bringing him breakfast, lunch and dinner. She read

him the evening news in the newspaper, Mr. Julies' eyes weren't so

good anymore. She rolled his wheelchair out onto the porch in the

morning and back into the house when it got late.

She expected no reward.

On that July 18th day, they were on the front porch as usual.

She was sitting next to him in her rocking chair, as she thumbed

through the daily newspaper. They carried on their usual small talk.

She had finished the first few pages and then she stopped abruptly.

"Hey, Unc! Their gonna tear down that pool hall!" she bellowed.
". . . The one you used to go to!"

"They're gonna tear it down? What fo'?" Mr. Julies asked.

"Says here they gonna make room for some luxury apartments,"
she said.

"Now ain't that just like the city: tear down a museum peice to
crowd an already crowded place," he said.

"Now, Unc. You know nothing happened in that pool hall but fights and all kinds of carrying on. So what if the city sees a little opportunity? 'Sides, you haven't been in that place in twenty years," she said.

"Yes, but a lot of good memories, a lot of good memories," he said, looking out into the passing cars in the street.

She continued to flip in the paper.

She stopped.

"Unc! How old are you?" she asked.

"You know how old I am," he answered.

Her eyes widened.

"Unc! Didn't you say you were a sailor during the great war?" she asked.

"You know that, child," he answered.

She sat up straight with the paper in her hand.

"Says here they interviewed a man in Washington, D.C. by the name of Jimmy Timmings. Says he was in the great war, like you, Unc! *A sailor.* It goes on to say that he claimed to be aboard a ship out in the middle of the Atlantic ocean, searching for submarines. The city is paying tribute to Black men who's story might have been lost but who made solid contributions during the war."

She looked at him. "Unc, this man is 105 years old!"

There was a noticeable silence.

She looked at him. "Didn't you say you were on a ship out in the Atlantic to?"

Mr. Julies looked away. Then he looked back at the street.

". . . Jimmy. He's still alive," he said quietly, and after a few moments.

"You knew him didn't you? You knew that man they interviewed. You were a part of those missions. You told me so: You launched off the coast of Massachusetts on board a huge vessel, bound for the

Atlantic. And you stayed out on the water for weeks, deep below the sea, among sharks, searching for enemy submarines."

Mr. Julies looked away again.

"Jimmy. That old son of a gun! I knew he was around somewhere," he said. "Did they find the others?"

"There were others?"

". . . Yes. There were four of us. Did they find the other two?" he asked.

"There's no mention of it here," she said, showing him the newspaper.

". . . Too bad. They must have gotten lost out there, somewhere," he said.

"Unc! You're a hero. They don't know about you but you deserve some of the credit, for the dives, just like this man in the paper!" she said.

"Nevermind, child. I ain't seeking no credit. I did my duty. That's all," he said.

"Unc, you did that and more!" she said.

"Take me into the house," he said after a few moments had passed.

"But Unc, it's only one thirty. You want to go in so early?" she asked.

"Yes. Take me in," he said.

"I hope what I said didn't upset you?" she asked.

"No. Not at all. Just take me inside," he said.

She stood up and put the newspaper into her rocking chair. She got behind his wheelchair and rolled him inside the house. There was a long hallway that lead into the main part of the house. His room was just off to the left in the hallway near the front door for easy access, exit and entrance.

She rolled him into his room and parked him so that his knees touched his bed. She turned on the t.v. set that was near the foot of his bed.

He didn't seem to notice.
She started for the door.
"I'll bring in your lunch in a moment," she said.
He didn't answer. He was very silent.

When she had left he stared at the window for a moment. The window was across his bed. He remained silent for several more minutes. There was a lamp table on the right side of his bed. It had a little drawer, almost unnoticeable beneath the lamp. He pulled open the drawer. There was a little book in it and he took it out. It was an old album full of pictures. He began to flip back and forth through the pictures. Finally, he stopped at a point midway through the album.

He began to mumble:

"There you are, Jimmy!: all *four* of us; standing proudly together before we sailed off to the Atlantic for that one month journey, eighty years ago. We weathered storms, and sharks and everything you could imagine in our dives, being so far from home and so far out in the ocean. I'm glad they found you, Jimmy. You can tell our story: the story that four men did their job and helped in this nations war effort. I don't know where the other two of you are, Jasper and Ryan, but I'm sure you would agree, we found no subs, but we found ourselves. We did what we could."

CHAPTER

T*WO*

Gloria entered the room with a tray of food, a ham sandwich, a cup of cold ice tea and a piece of fruit. She sat the tray on a flat area at the front of his wheelchair. She turned his chair towards the t.v.

"Enjoy your lunch, Unc," she said. "I'll be back to check on you soon."

She started out. She noticed the small album on the lamp table. She came back into the room. "What's this, Unc?"

She picked up the album and began flipping through it.

She looked at him. "Uncle Julies, some of these pictures must be sixty or seventy years old. She continued to flip through them. ". . . Their soldiers."

She looked at him at the t.v.

He had not started his lunch.

Her eyes widened. She came around to the front of him and stood between himself and the t.v.

She knelt down. ". . . Their *you!*"

She flipped through the pictures some more. "Uncle Julies, these are pictures of you! And others! And some of these resemble that man that was in the paper! How long have you had this?"

". . . A long time he said," he said, finally.

She closed the album.

"Their priceless, Uncle Julies. You saw the picture out front and it brought on the memories. But that's okay."

She put the album back on the lamp table. "Keep it close to you. It's a good thing."

She gave him a pat on the back. "Enjoy your lunch, Unc. I'll see you after a while."

She went to the door, opened it and exited.

She was washing dishes that afternoon. She was busy as she always was taking care of the house. The daily paper continued to come into her sight as it lay innocently on the kitchen table.

She tried to ignore it: but she couldn't. It seemed to continue to stare at her as she continued to stare at it.

Finally, she gave in.

She went to the paper and picked it up, flipped to the section where the old man had served thousands of miles away out in the Atlantic, looking for enemy submarines.

The article was a reprint of the interview that appeared in _The Washington Post_ three days earlier.

She went to the phone and called long distance to _The Post_ and was connected to it's editor. She mentioned that there was another man that was also on that ship that cruised out in the Atlantic on that faithful journey: and it was her uncle! Her call was met with much resistance and skepticism around the editorial offices of _The Post_ but she answered every question right, including the date the ship sailed, the name of the ship, 'The Atlas', the date it returned, July 18, 1942; making it the eightieth anniversary of it's returning; and the names of some of the men aboard; Jasper Johnson and Ryan Watts. My uncle was last to come up. He has mentioned those men from time to time. They were on that same ship as my uncle. You found Mr. Jimmy. He was in the papers. But my uncle was the last to come up. Did they ever find those other two divers that were on board?"

They were suddenly astonished.

"Who is this?" asked someone from the Post after several seconds had passed.

Gloria could tell that the man was a bit unnerved by her call.

"My name is Gloria Caldwell. I'm here in Fulton County Georgia, that's just outside Atlanta," she said.

"You say you have an uncle that was on that dive lady? That means he's have to be over a hundred years old now," the man said.

"Yes, that's my Uncle Julies. And he's a hundred and six, for your information. And he participated in that dive. I have photographs of he and that man you interviewed; standing together; smiling at the camera, just before they left on that voyage back in '42. They were pals. All of them were! My uncle was a hero! He was out there in those waters for more than twelve hours! And I dare you to question the man you interviewed about who my uncle is and what he meant to him during that war," she said.

"Give me your phone number," the man on the other end said.

Gloria belted out her ten digits including the area code.

The man continued: "I'll call you back later. And this better not be a prank or I can have you arrested for making these kinds of calls."

"Do what you have to do, Sir. I'll be waiting," Gloria said.

And she hung up. She paused for a second or two.

She looked back at the room her elderly uncle was waiting and then she looked satisfied. She crossed the hallway to his room and found him having finished his lunch. He had fallen asleep, the tray was half empty, and the t.v. was still playing.

She picked up the tray from the front of the wheelchair and looked at him. "Like I said, Unc, you're a hero; a natural born hero. And a brave man. And all the world should know it. They know about your friends, they should know about you to."

She turned and quietly left the room, leaving the door slightly open as she returned his tray to the kitchen.

CHAPTER

T*HREE*

4:00 p.m.

It had been no more than an hour or two when the phone

rang. Gloria was reading in the living room near the front of the

house. She put the book she was reading aside, ran down the hallway

to her bedroom across from her uncles room and picked up the

phone.

"Hello!" she said.

"Hello. Miss Cauldwell? Charlie Watkins here from *The Washington post.* We spoke this morning," the man on the other end said.

"Yes, Sir. How are you?"

"Fine, Miss Cauldwell. As I mentioned, I'm a reporter here at the paper. I gave your story to my bosses and they contacted the man we interviewed for that submarine story we ran today. The man we interviewed stumbled. But he seemed to remember your uncle, Julies Hampton, was it?" he asked.

"Yes, Uncle Julies," she said.

"You say, he's a hundred and six?"

"Yes."

"Then those *two* are the last of the four divers," the man said.

"What happened to the other two?" Gloria asked.

"I'm afraid they are no longer with us," the man said.

"I see," Gloria said.

The reporter paused.

"You say you live just outside Atlanta, Miss Cauldwell?" he asked.

"Yes, Sir."

"I just had a brainstorm. What do you say I came to visit this 'Johnny-come-lately' uncle of yours, just to hear his side of the story. Might be of interest to our readers to know that there is a supplementary: another survivor of those treacherous dives into the deep Atlantic. Not only would we have one hero, we'd have two. What do you say?" he asked.

"I'd welcome it, Mr. Watkins. I'd welcome it," she said, calmly.

"Good. I'm just a reporter here and I haven't been with the paper for very long. But I think I know a good story when I see one. This should do wonders for me. And it does have great human interest. Let me see if I can fix it up with my boss. I'll call you back later this evening," the reporter said.

"Fine, Sir. I'll wait," she said.

They hung up the phone.

Gloria paused for a moment. She felt good about the way things were going. She looked across the hallway towards her uncle's room. It would be about his supper time in two hours and she went into the kitchen to began preparing for it.

CHAPTER

F*OUR*

5:30 P.M. same day

"**M**y boss has cleared me to fly down to Georgia to see you,

Miss Cauldwell. Your uncle is one hundred and six. I might want a

statement or two about the voyage from him. You think he feels up

to it?" the reporter, Mr. Watkins asked.

"My uncle, Mr. Julies can out talk the best of them. You just ask anybody in the neighborhood," Gloria answered.

"Good. We want to hear his side of the story and compare it to his friend, our interviewee, Mr. Jimmy Timmings, just to get a different perspective on the same issue. My boss calls it voyage part one; and voyage part two," the reporter said.

"You just come right on. We'll be waiting," Gloria said.

8:30 a.m. the next day,

The phone rang again.

It was the reporter.

It was the next day, the 19th, and he had arrived in Atlanta.

"Miss Cauldwell? Charlie Watkins here. I'm here in Fulton County. It's a beautiful place. I have your address. I took a cab from Hartsfield Airport. According to my driver I'm just around the corner from you. Do I still have permission to come over?" the reporter asked.

"You have it, Sir. It's the light green wood frame house at the end of Peach Street. You can't miss it," she said.

"I should be there shortly," the reporter said.

"Come right on, Sir," Gloria said.

She hung up the phone.

She looked at her uncles's room feeling a bit gratified that he was about to get his just due. She went into the kitchen and began to do chores around the house.

8:45 a.m.

There was a knock at the front door. Gloria was still in the kitchen. She was preparing her Uncle's breakfast, ham and eggs. Juice.

She went to the door to answer it. She opened the front door.

There was a tall, slender, caucasian man standing in her doorway. He was dressed in an all white suit; white coat, white shirt, white patent leather shoes and a black tie. He was neatly turned out. He looked young. To her, he looked only to be about in his late twenties or early thirties. He had a briefcase in his right hand and he smiled broadly as the door swung open.

He stuck out his hand.

"Miss Cauldwell?" he asked.

"Yes?" she asked.

"I'm Charles Watkins from *The Washington Post.* We've spoken. Nice to meet you," he said, friendlily.

She accepted his friendly gesture and shook his hand.

"Nice to meet you also, Mr. Watkins. You've come a long way. I hope what we have here is worth your while," she said.

"I'm sure it is, Miss Cauldwell. Your uncle's story sounds very intriguing, and a natural addition to what we've already reported in our yesterdays edition," he said.

Gloria took two steps towards him and came onto the porch.

She walked over to the side of him.

"Mr. Watkins, there is something I must tell you. My uncle is finishing up his breakfast right now. However, he's in a wheelchair. And when he comes out here don't be surprised when he finds out who you are and where you came from and that he balks a bit. I haven't told him you were coming. Just ignore him a little: at first," she admitted.

"He doesn't know I'm here, Mam?" he asked.

"No. But when you ask him about these things, be a little kind to him about it. He seldomn discusses them: even to me," she said.

"I understand," he said.

"I'll go get him," she said.

She entered his room. He was just about to finish his breakfast. His wheelchair, as usual, was pushed up against his bed his knees touching it.

She came to the back side of him.

"Uncle Julies, are you finished eating?" she asked him.

"Yes. Finished. Gonna watch a little t.v.," he said.

She took his tray from the front of his chair and sat it on top of the lamp table. She took the handles of his wheelchair and slowly spun him around so that he faced the door.

She knelt in front of him.

"Feel like company?" she asked.

". . . Company?"

"Yes. You have a visitor."

"Me? Who?"

She stood up.

"Why don't you just come outside and meet him," she said, walking to the back of his chair.

She rolled him out of the room, turned right and exited the front door onto the front porch. There standing on the front steps, fanning himself with a handkerchief was Mr. Watkins.

Mr. Watkins put away his handkerchief and flashed a ready smile. He offered his hand.

"Mr. Hampton! So nice to meet you, Sir!" he said.

Gloria came between the two men.

"Uncle Julies, this is Mr. Charlie Watkins. Mr. Watkins, this is the uncle I told you about - from the war: Uncle Julies," she said.

Mr. Hampton seemed a but stunned by the intrusion but from his wheelchair he offered his hand in return.

She looked at her uncle. "I hope you don't mind, Uncle Julies, but I invited Mr. Watkins here. He's from _The Washington post,_ the big newspaper up there. Remember the article about your friend and comrade Jimmy, the one who you served with? Well I thought you should get some credit to. After all, you were both on the same boat that day, and you were both divers, looking for submarines."

The young reporter looked admiringly at Mr. Hampton.

"So that's why I'm here, Mr. Hampton. Needless to say, we were quite stunned to find out about you. We had already interviewed your comrade and had gotten his story. When we found out about you, we became very excited to know that there was another man out there that had gone through the _same_ experience. We want to hear your side of the story to," the young reporter said.

Mr. Hampton looked away.

"That was a long time ago, Sonny. If'n you heard one story, maybe you heard the _whole_ story," he said.

The young reported knelt in front of his wheelchair.

"But maybe not, Sir. All you men, you were heroes out there. All of you deserve to be known to the public and recognized for bravery for your service, not pushed under the rug," he said.

"Push it under the rug," Mr. Hampton said.

"I hope not," the young reporter said.

The young reporter came to his feet.

"Maybe you need a little more sun, Unc?" Gloria said.

She pushed his wheelchair a little closer to the end of the large porch.

She got another chair from the other end of the porch and sat it next to Mr. Hamptons. "Won't you sit down, Mr. Watkins? You two should get acquainted, despite my uncles ineptness."

He sat in the chair next to Mr. Hampton. From his inside coat pocket he took out a small pad and pen.

He looked at Mr. Hampton.

"Mr. Hampton, I can understand your obvious criticism about all of this; that means your 'stand offishness', after all it has been a long time. But this story belongs to the people; people should know about this. You were out in the middle of the ocean. The boat was no bigger than this porch. There was thought to be enemy subs, *German subs,* in the area where you were. Yet, you and three other men risked their lives, diving into the sea on a mission that turned out to be, quite bogus. Report was: you found no submarines. Nothing that could threaten the eastern seaboard of the United States was found. Two men drowned. You and Mr. Timmings were the only survivors. And yet, after your return nothing was said about the mission. It was as if it never happened: and was unimportant: scratched from the record; not being mentioned, except in bars and idle conversations, disappearing into folklore," the young reporter asked.

And then he concluded: "And our interviewee, Mr. Timmings. He took all the credit. What happened out there? I want to hear *your* side?" the young reporter asked.

The old man paused.

"I got no feelings about it," he said. "It's been gone this long, why bring it up now?"

"Because it *should* be, that's why, Mr. Hampton. No matter the length of time, this should be brought to the surface. I knew it when I interviewed Mr. Timmings, and I know it now," the reporter said.

"I'm older than he. It's a waste of time. Who'd be interested?" Mr. Hampton asked, not looking at the man.

"You'd be surprised, Mr. Hampton," the reporter said.

Mr. Hampton turned away and giggled a bit.

"Yeah, I might be," he said.

The reporter looked at Mr. Hampton.

"So how about it, Sir? Can you shed more light on that diving mission you and three others went on - only two coming back, for this eager-beaver, who could use a good story?" the young reporter asked.

There was a pause. The reporter looked at Mr. Hampton. Mr. Hampton's eyes appeared reflective and glassy: even sad.

"Like I said, Son, that was a long time ago," Mr. Hampton said.

"Bring it back, Sir. The world should know about this," the reporter said.

"There is nothing to know," Mr. Hampton said.

He leaned back into his wheelchair. He stared at the young reporter. "Where did you say you come from, Son?"

"Washington, D.C., Sir."

"I'm afraid it's a long trip for nothing, Son," Mr. Hampton said.

"But it can't be, Sir. I need to put a resolution to this story. My interviewing Mr. Timmings was appreciated, but after hearing from you and your niece here, I know it's only half finished. I'll ask you the same thing I asked him. Why did four men dive into the ocean and only two came up? Twenty four hours ago I thought that was the end of the story. And now I get a call and I've found you. Where were you? Why were *you* the last to come up? And why were you missing for over a day? And how did you survive for over a day out in the open waters?" the reporter asked.

Mr. Hampton looked away. It was quiet for a few more moments. Mr. Hampton turned his head completely away from the man.

Gloria was still standing in back of his wheelchair.

"Uncle Julies? You okay?" she asked him, leaning forward to look at him.

Mr. Hampton seemed disturbed.

". . . I think so. Take me inside," he said, quietly and after a few seconds had passed.

The young reporter looked up at Gloria her hands on both the wheelchairs handles.

"Did I say something?" he asked, quietly.

Gloria slowly and gently maneuvered her uncle's wheelchair towards the front door.

"It's just his way when he doesn't want to talk anymore. He just clams up," she said.

She rolled his wheelchair to the front door and stopped.

He put his hands on the wheels to stop his forward progress.

She leaned over to him. "What is it, Uncle Julies?"

There was another pause as he held onto both wheels firmly with his hands.

He stared at the door and didn't look back.

". . . *Tomorrow,*" he said, under his breath.

The young reporter stood up from his chair. He walked to the back of the wheelchair where Gloria stood.

He pulled her to one side.

". . . Did he say what I thought he said?" he asked her.

"I think so. You can come again tomorrow. But no guarantees on how he'll react to you. He says one thing one minute, and does something quite different the next," she explained.

"I'll take my chances," the young reporter said.

Mr. Hampton began to roll his wheels towards the front door and finally into the house where he disappeared.

Gloria looked back at the man.

". . . The same time? Eight thirty?" she asked, quietly.

"Fine. See you then," he said, just as quiet.

Gloria turned and walked inside, closing the door behind her.

The young reporter put his pad and pen back into his coat pocket. He walked back to his chair, sat, took out his phone and called a taxi.

CHAPTER

F*IVE*
8:30 A.M.
THE FOLLOWING MORNING

He turned up at the doorway of Gloria and Mr. Hampton's

promptly at 8:30 a.m. sharp. He had spent the night at a local

hotel; had gotten a good nights sleep and had changed into a bluish

business suit. He then took at taxi back to Gloria and Mr.

Hampton's house.

She answered with a pleasant smile at the doorway.

"Well, good morning, Mr. Watkins. I wasn't sure if you'd come back after our abrupt ending of the interview yesterday," she said.

"I had to come back. There is nothing I find more intriguing or important than this," he said.

"Have a seat, Mr. Watkins. Had your coffee?"

"No, Mam. I came right over," he said.

"I'll get that for you," she said. Then in the doorway she asked: "Cream or sugar?"

"Cream," the reporter said.

"Coming up," Gloria said, then she disappeared into the house.

———————————————

She reappeared a few moments later with a coffee cup on a saucer.

The cream was on the saucer: and a spoon.

He looked at the skies as he mixed his coffee.

"Beautiful day isn't it, Miss Cauldwell?" he asked.

"We have a lot of beautiful days around here, Mr. Watkins," she said. "But a lot of times it's mixed with rain."

He took a sip from his coffee.

"Every day should be this beautiful," he said.

Gloria closed the front door, returned and sat in another chair on the opposite end of the porch.

He took another sip from his coffee and looked across the porch at her. "Where is, Mr. Hampton?"

"I just gave him his breakfast. I'll go fetch him in a minute," she said.

The reporter took another sip of his coffee.

"I'm enjoying our talk. Let him take his time," he said.

She looked at him curiously.

"You really think my uncle's story is going to be something, Mr. Watkins?" she asked.

"I think so. Your uncle is one of two survivors on that ship. You have made that clear and he has confirmed it. What happened to the others? They were never found, except for Mr. Timmings, pulled up from the sea, gagging for air from his half empty air tank after only about two hours. Your uncle was gone for over a day, found in the open sea. Mr. Timmings said so in our last interview. They said he was as calm and well fed as could be. What happened out there? And why was your uncle so terribly *lucky?*" the reporter asked. Then concluded: "If I can get to the bottom of it, *this* story could prove more intriguing than any I've covered this year!"

Mr. Hampton appeared in the doorway.

"You'all talking 'bout me? I can always tell when someone is talkin' 'bout me," he said.

He looked rather feeble. He had a blanket wrapped across his legs. He began turning the wheels on his wheelchair to come to the front porch.

Gloria stood up abruptly.

"Uncle, what are you doing out here? Did you finish your breakfast?" she asked, walking over to him.

"I finished it."

He noticed the reporter, Mr. Watkins, sitting in he same chair he had previously sat.

Mr. Watkins, the young reporter, stood up.

"Good morning, Mr. Hampton. Nice to see you today, Sir," he said.

"You still here?" Mr. Hampton asked. "What did ja' do: spend the night on the porch?"

"No, Sir. Actually I spent the night in a hotel room, right down the street from here, courtesy of my newspaper," Mr. Watkins said.

"Well, I said you could come back and you did," Mr. Hampton said.

Gloria took the initiative.

"Why don't the two of you go out under the shade of the oak tree? It's cooler than this porch and you can talk there?" she asked.

"'Bout what? Seems to me we've covered everything," Mr. Hampton said.

"It would mean a lot to me, Sir. Your story. It would mean a lot to my readers," the reporter said.

There was a wheelchair friendly *'ramp'* next to the stairs.

"Well, you waisting yo' time not mine. I was going out there anyway," Mr. Hampton said.

He looked at Gloria. "Push me out there."

Gloria went to the back of the wheelchair and began to push him towards the ramp and to the end of the porch. The ramp was about three feet steep.

Mr. Watkins took a couple of steps towards them.

He looked at Mr. Hampton and then at Gloria.

"If you don't mind: it would be my pleasure?" he asked.

Gloria stepped aside and Mr. Watkins, the young reporter, took the reins of the wheelchair from her. He rolled him down the ramp and to the mushroom shaped and shady oak tree to his right. He parked the wheelchair there near the trunk and in back of the tree away from the morning sun.

"Thank you, Mr. Watkins," she said from the porch. "You two have a pleasant conversation."

CHAPTER

S^{IX}

M_{r.} Watkins, the young reporter, took out his pad
and pen from his coat pocket.

He sat at the trunk of the tree in front of Mr. Hampton's
wheelchair.

"Why don't we start at the beginning, Mr. Hampton? You men
were out there chasing submarines: something that ultimately they
found did not even exist?" he asked, looking at Mr. Hampton in all
earnesty.

Mr. Hampton paused.

"I promised you something, Boy, and I'm gonna give you
something. . . you do what you gotta do when you gotta do it," Mr.
Hampton said.

"What do you mean, Sir?"

"We were called to duty. They suspected that there were enemy
subs, German subs, waddling around out there in the area, plotting
to cut off our shipping lanes and trade with foreign allies: our
friends. Two ships, in fact, had mysteriously disappeared: sank out in
the middle of the Atlantic with no trace," Mr. Hampton said. "Those
ships had men aboard: good men, I'm sho', trying to deliver goods or
supplies to the allies. But something stopped them."

"In the end they said it was weather, that caused those two ships to go down. It was stormy that time of the year. That's what Mr. Timmings said. So they needed men to go out and find, or at least substantiate what we were thinking here in the States. Submarines," the reporter said.

"Precisely, my friend," Mr. Hampton said. "Me, 'Jimmy', or Mr. Timmings, as you call him: Ryan, and Jasper was the ones they chose to go out. We were all expert swimmers: they knew that from training exercises we had performed off shore for the Army Air Corps at our Base in New York. Ryan and Jasper, I understand is no longer around, but I'm sure Jimmy made it clear that we were all hand picked for the assignment. Jimmy, Ryan and me were all colored guys: Jasper was the only white fella. Too bad Ryan and Jasper were such good swimmers, they'd probably be here today."

Mr. Hampton was not looking at him.

The reported jotted down what Mr. Hampton had said.

Then he stopped writing.

He continued to stare at his writing pad.

He looked at Mr. Hampton.

"So there you were: out in the middle of the Atlantic; no doubt in choppy waters," he said.

"Yes. The ship rocked back and forth," Mr. Hampton said. "It was scary, I don't mind saying."

"How big was this ship?"

"'Bout as big as that porch," Mr. Hamton said, pointing at the house.

"That's about the size Mr. Timmings said," the young reporter said.

He paused.

The young reporter looked at Mr. Hampton with wonder. "How many men were on that tiny vessel?"

"'Bout twelve in all. That is to say twelve went out: only ten came back," Mr. Hampton said.

"You were one of those ten," the reporter said.

". . . Yes."

". . . And so was Mr. Timmings," the reporter said.

". . . Yes."

The reporter wrote down what had been said.

He looked back to Mr. Hampton with curious eyes.

"Ever thought about him, Sir? Mr. Timmings? Your friend? Has he ever crossed your mind in all these ensuing years?" he asked.

"'Course, all those men has crossed my mind. But what could I do 'sides think of 'em? It's over. It's a done deal," Mr. Hampton said."

"It's funny, Mr. Timmings often couldn't recall your name in my interview," the reporter said.

"It's okay. It has been a long time," Mr. Hampton said.

Mr. Hampton looked sad. And disturbed.

The young reporter sighed. He folded up his notes and put them into his pocket. He put his pen there also.

"Mr. Hampton, it's been a great interview today. But I suspect you want to be left alone," he said.

"You're very perceptive, boy. You stirring up things that been on the back burner for a great many years," Mr. Hampton said.

"I apologize for that. Still, Mr. Hampton, there seems some missing links here: another part of this brave story you've given me: and don't get me wrong, it is a brave story. But I don't feel I've gotten to the bottom of it," Mr. Watkins said.

". . . Bottom, son? Whatcha mean?" Mr. Hampton asked.

The young reporter looked at him with all earnest.

"I've asked this question and I'll ask it again. Why did you luck out and survive the dive when two of your comrads never came up? What happened?" he asked.

Mr. Hampton looked away.

". . . I was Somewhere, boy. Somewhere," he answered.

Both men were silent for a moment.

Mr. Hampton called for Gloria. "Hey, girl?!"

Gloria appeared on the front porch.

Mr. Hampton adjusted his chair until he faced her. "I'm ready to come in."

The young reporter stood up.

He faced the older man.

". . . Somewhere, Mr. Hampton? Where is somewhere?" the reporter asked.

Mr. Hampton looked at the young reporter standing over him.

". . . Kindly roll me up the ramp," he said.

The young reporter took the wheelchair by it's handles and rolled Mr. Hampton to the ramp. He turned him backwards and pulled up the three feet to the porch.

Gloria took the handles from the young reporter and turned him to face the door.

Mr. Watkins, the young reporter, came around to the front of him.

He extended his hand to Mr. Hampton.

"Thank you, Sir."

He patted the notes he'd made that were in his coat pocket. "It's been a pleasure. I think I have what I need. Take care of yourself."

"You ain't got nothing."

"I beg your pardon, Sir?"

"You got what Jimmy told you. He always was a half talker."

"Come again?"

"That's exactly what I'm talking about: come again. Tomorrow," Mr. Hampton said.

"You really want me to, Sir?" the young reporter asked.

"I said so didn't I?"

Mr. Hampton began to wheel his chair towards the door.

Gloria looked back to the innocent reporter standing in back of them with his mouth open.

She shrugged her shoulders.

"He said come back. That means three talks, Mr. Watkins. You must have made *some* impression. Is 8:00 okay?"

"Sounds fine," Mr. Watkins answered, surprised at the extra time.

"Good. I'll see you in the morning," she said.

"Yes, Mam. In the morning," he said.

She took the helm of his wheelchair and rolled the now silent Mr. Hampton inside the house, closing the door behind her.

For the second straight day he went over to the side of the porch and called a cab.

CHAPTER

S*EVEN*

8:00 a.m. the following morning July 20th

He found himself rolling Mr. Hampton down the ramp and

into the yard. He rolled him to the same oak tree and it's shade and

maneuvered him so that he could face the road.

"It's another beautiful day, Sir," Mr. Watkins, the young reporter said.

"Fine day, son," Mr. Hampton said.

"Is that okay with you, Mr. Hampton?" the young reporter asked him, settling his chair under the tree.

"Fine, boy. But I don't know why you waisting yo' time: and mine," Mr. Hampton said.

"Maybe because I admire you, Mr. Hampton," he said.

"You admire *me?* I can think of a lot better heroes, son," Mr. Hampton said.

Just then, Gloria appeared on the front porch with a tray. It had a large picture on it and two glasses. He noticed a small tray of cubed ice on it as well.

"Refreshments for you two gentlemen. Cold lemonade. It might get hot out here," she said, walking down the stairs.

She sat the tray on a level part of Mr. Hampton's wheelchair, where he normally ate his breakfast.

Mr. Watkins stood up and helped her arrange the tray on the front of the wheelchair.

"You didn't have to do that, Miss Cauldwell," he said.

"Oh, yes I did. You're not from around here, Mr. Watkins, and let me tell you some days it can get awfully hot," she said. "Now you just enjoy and if you need more just holler."

"Thank you, Mam," Mr. Watkins said.

Gloria turned away and headed back onto the porch and into the house.

Mr. Watkins poured himself a glass of lemonade and then poured a glass for Mr. Hampton.

Mr. Hampton didn't seem interested.

He looked at Mr. Watkins.

"She's just buttering you up. She figure if she's nice to you you'll be nice to me, and I'll open up to you a little more," he said.

"You mean you haven't already?"

The young reporter took a swallow of his lemonade. "What don't I know, Sir? What haven't you opened up to me?"

Mr. Hampton looked away.

"Pour some more lemonade," Mr. Hampton said.

The young reporter did. Then he sat on the ground, took another swallow and leaned up against the tree.

Mr. Hampton rested back into his chair.

He began to talk.

". . . There was twelve us out out there," he began. "Twelve men on a boat no bigger than that front porch. Yes, the waters were choppy. But we had a job to do: a big job. They feared something or someone was cutting off our shipping lanes, as we sent and received supplies from our friends overseas. We were sent out there to find out what it was. They thought it was submarines: German Submarines. But as it turned out, we found no submarines, no foreign ships, no nothing. It was a banner year out in the Atlantic. Many storms off the coast of Africa came through. Hurricanes. And as it turned out, all the boats carrying supplies were sank by natural causes: winds and rains! It's amazing that we in our tiny excusion ship made it back to the east coast, where they found us tired and hungry, after weeks out in the Atlantic, and we were escorted back to the base in New York."

"They thought you had failed?" the reporter asked, taking another swallow from his glass.

"I guess. They might had been better off. They were going to send our subs into the area but the ocean can be miles deep, they thought it was too risky," Mr. Hampton said.

"So you and your men took all the risks. And found nothing," Mr. Watkins said.

". . . Yes. Except. . . "

Mr. Hampton stopped.

The young reporter sat up straight.

"Except what, Mr. Hampton?" the young reporter said.

". . . Except a very large stone rock, miles deep beneath the surface, on the ocean floor," Mr. Hampton said.

Mr. Watkins sat the glass of lemonade on the ground.

". . . A large stone rock?"

"Yes. And it was not there by chance. It was *man made*," Mr. Hampton said.

"I large rock; two miles deep on the ocean floor and it was man made? How? How could you tell it was man made, Sir?" he asked.

"It had *steps* on it. *Steps:* cut out of that rock, as plain as the steps leading up to the house," Mr. Hampton said.

The young reporter took out his pad and pen.

"Go on, Mr. Hampton," he said.

". . . Maybe I've said enough," Mr. Hampton said.

"I don't think you've said enough, Sir," the young boy said.

Mr. Hampton continued.

"Yes. It was steps. Somehow, in the choppy waters, I became disoriented. I began to swim without direction not knowing where I was going. When I got my bearings I realized that I was miles beneath the surface. That's when I saw it: the rock. Yet it seemed fragmented: as if it was part of a larger rock that fallen in that place. I knew my air tank was getting low. My guage showed only about two hours left. So I didn't have time for a careful examination. I turned upwards and that's when I saw something even more spectacular than the first," Mr. Hampton said.

"And what was that?" the reporter asked him.

". . . A boy: a young boy, an aquaboy, *swimming,* thousands of feet below the surface of the open ocean like it was nothing. He had goggles over his eyes, fins on both his feet and no air tank, only what appeared to be a giant *sea shell* on his back," Mr. Hampton recalled, his eyes wide.

". . . A boy? You sure it was none of your men?" the reporter asked.

"I know it wasn't. Without air? I knew right away that it wasn't one of us. He had a bow and arrow in his hands," Mr. Hampton answered.

". . . A bow and arrow?" the reporter asked, without movement.

"Yes. And a batch of arrows in a pouch next to the sea shell on his back."

The young reporter began to jot down everything that was said.

He looked up at Mr. Hampton.

"Why the bow and arrow?" he asked.

"He seemed to be catching fish, putting them on his sidebelt!" Mr. Hampton said.

". . . Now let me get this straight: a young boy out in the middle of the sea, catching fish with a bow and arrow," the reporter said.

"Yes."

"Then what happened?" the young reporter asked.

"He came after me."

"He saw you?"

"He pointed his bow and arrow at me. This aquaboy seemed as startled to see me as I was to see him," Mr. Hampton said.

The young reporters eyes were wide with skepticism but he continued to jot down what Mr. Hampton had said.

"Then what?" he asked, looking back at Mr. Hampton.

"I held up my hands, of course. High!" Mr. Hampton said. "I had never seen anything like that befo.'"

"Obviously, he let you go," the reporter said.

"Yeah, but not befo' taking me through a tunnel that led up to a dry cave-like place. When we surfaced I saw twenty foot waterfalls coming out of the side of the caves hundreds of feet from where we were. I couldn't believe what I was seeing!" Mr. Hampton said.

The reporter seemed wrapped up in Mr. Hampton's story.

"Go on, Mr. Hampton," he said, more concerned with the man than his notes.

"Well, Suh," Mr. Hampton continued. "He lets me drop my hands. And he took off his goggles. I took off my goggles. I thought, this boy couldn't be no more than sixteen or seventeen years old. I thought, what was he doing swimming around out there?"

"*W*ho are you?" he asked me.

"Me? My name is Julies Hampton," I told him.

"What you doing here? Where are you from?" he asked.

"I could ask you the same thing," I said to him. *"Who* **are** *you?"*

With his wide fins on his feet, a giant shell on his back, he circled me round and round.

When he reached the front of me again he said:

"They call me Jeremy," the boy answered.

Mr. Hampton leaned backwards into his chair.

It seemed as if it was an important moment. Mr. Hampton faultered a bit.

"He put the arrow to my throat. He seemed to be sizing me up. I must have passed the grade: he didn't stick that arrow into me," Mr. Hampton said.

Mr. Hampton began to twiddle his thumbs as if in deep thought.

"The sea boy continued speaking: *I live here. This is my home,*" he said.

"*In a cave?*" I asked him, confused. "*At the bottom of the sea?*"

"*No. Over yonder.*"

"Well Mr. Reporter, he pointed to his left near the end of the cave."

"*There are more caves,*" the young boy said. "*More of us.*"

"*Us?*" I asked him.

"*Yes. My people.*"

"*I can't believe it. We must be ten thousand feet below the surface of the open sea!*"

I took a step in his direction. "*You've got to tell me what this is all about? Where am I?*"

"He held up his bow and arrow to my throat again. I backed away. I held up my hands again."

"*No need for that. I'm sorry. I didn't mean it the way it sounded.*"

Mr. Hampton looked away. "Well, Mr. Reporter, after a few moments he seemed to have finished 'sizing me up.' He lowered his bow and arrow. Finally."

"*Your name is Julies?*" he asked.

"*Yes.*"

"*Where are you from, Julies?*"

"*From the surface, two miles above where we are now.*"

"*You float on top of the water?*" he asked.

"*No. From a continent called America. Have you heard of it?*"

"I have not."

"You have never heard of America?" **I asked him.**

"No."

"How long have you been here?" **I asked.**

"A very long time. We are an old civilization that came from the surface like you. But this is our home now," **he said.**

"Then he looked at me curiously."

"You have very dark skin. You must be from Africa, not this America, you speak of. Your skin is very dark, like mine. We have many here who's heritage is from Africa," **he said.**

"Later, I thought that was why he suddenly became friendsly, because of our common skin color."

Mr. Hampton looked away then back at the young reporter who had resumed taking notes.

"Well, for the first time the boy smiled at me. He approached me.

"It is good to welcome one from the dark continent to be among us. We welcome you among us. I won't ask how you got here. You are here now, and another only makes us stronger," **he said.**

"He squeezed my arms."

"Would you like to meet the others?" **he asked.**

"The others?"

"My people," **he said.**

"Well, I'm here now. I may as well," **I said.**

CHAPTER

EIGHT

The young reporter, Mr. Watkins, had become

enthralled, baffled and intrigued about Mr. Hampton's story, so

much so, that he had stood up and began to pace back and forth next

to the tree.

He knelt down in front of Mr. Hampton.

"Sir, you mean to tell me that you were on the floor of the ocean, met a boy there who was fishing, two thousand miles from land, two miles beneath the surface in a cave, and he befriended you?" he asked.

". . . Yes."

"That's almost out of the question: hard to believe!" the young reporter said.

"**A**nd don't forget about the *others* he mentioned," Mr.

Hampton said.

The young reporter sat back into his spot under the tree.

"I haven't forgotten them. Where were they?"

Mr. Hampton leaned backwards into his chair.

He resumed his story.

"I'm getting to that," Mr. Hampton said.

The reporter took out his pad and pen he had sat on the ground and began to write.

Mr. Hampton sat deeper into his chair.

"We began to walk towards what seemed to be a small

puddle of water near the end of the cave."

The agua-boy spoke up first.

"Does the thing on your back give you air?" the boy asked me.

"Yes," I told him. *"It supplies me with compressed air so that I can breath underwater - through my mouth. It is an air tank."*

I showed him the mouthpiece.

"You will need it. We are going down there," he said.

"We are going down there? Why?"

"To my home: the place I told you about," he said.

"Is it far? I mean, how will you *catch air?"*

He pointed to the giant shell on his back.

"Through this. It is much like your air tank on your back, except when we reach air, it restores itself: like now; air is trapped within it's confines and I can breath through this."

The boy showed him what was a simple hose that connected to the sea shell on his back. The hose went to his mouth.

"Ingenious," I told him.

He put the hose into his mouth.

"As I got to know the boy better, I noticed that I had began to let down my defenses. I had never seen such things, such innovation, such wonders. And I sensed that he was also curious about me. I was beginning to wonder what I would see next."

The boy put on his goggles. I hesitated a bit. Naturally. Yet he was very encouraging.

"Please come. It is okay," he said.

"I still wasn't sure if I would go through with what he had in mind. Yet I found myself putting on the goggles, and my mouthpiece to my air tank into my mouth."

Mr. Hampton paused. He seemed to recall their next moves with some difficulty.

He twiddled his thumbs as he continued on: "**F**eet first, the boy dove into the small puddle. I went in after him in the same manner. I was used to these procedures. Almost immediately, I saw a tunnel, a narrow one that led into the same direction as the tunnel that led them to the cave. It wasn't long and I could almost see to the end of it ahead of the boy. Soon, we were coming out of that tunnel. Schools of fish of a specie I hadn't seen befo' passed beneath us."

Mr. Hampton looked away. "What I saw next I will never forget. The boy came out first ahead of me. Then I emerged."

Mr. Hampton seemed flabbergasted.

"**A**s I looked past the fish and beyond the murky waters, I noticed there was a vast city beneath me! That's right: *a vast city!* We seemed to be thousands of feet above it. It was like being in an airplane and flying over it. There were clusters of buildings! Clusters! And they were centered in cicles that extended to the outbounds of the city itself. Then there was another circle. Then a larger circle beyond it! Yet, the buildings seemed small, no more than two or three stories high. The 'circles' that surrounded the city I assume today were only *suburbs,* if you will, that lead outwardly until there was nothing."

The reporter, Charlie Watkins, had long stopped taking notes.

"You weren't seeing things, Sir? *A city:* thousands of feet on the floor of the ocean?" he asked Mr. Hampton. "You weren't seeing things, Sir?"

"What do you mean 'was I seeing things?' I saw it as plain as I'm looking at you now," Mr. Hampton said.

"Nothing implied, Sir. But sometimes the depths of the ocean is like being out in the desert. It can play tricks on you," the reporter said.

"There was no tricks," Mr. Hampton said.

"Then do you know what you just described to me?"

"What?"

". . . Atlantis. The long lost city that supposingly sank below the depths of the ocean by an earthquake thousands of years ago, never to be seen again," the reporter said.

"How can that be? Seems it would be totally destroyed," Mr. Hampton said.

"You would think so. But people have been searching for it for centuries and no one has seen a trace of it: until now, if this is for real," he reporter said.

"'Course it's for real! I've no reason to lie to you," Mr. Hampton snapped.

The young reporter started to write again.

"Go on, Mr. Hampton," he said.

"The aquaboy signaled me with his finger and we began to descend. Bubbles of air coming out of our mouths, we landed at one of the lowered buildings on the far end of the city. It was only about two stories high. There were side walks there, many sidewalks, that seemed to go throughout the city. The buildings, though small by todays standards, seemed tall once we had reached ground level. We actually entered the building he seemed to be aiming for. It seemed to be a bar or a pub: there was a counter still intact and iron chairs and tables with green mold and seaweed on them that I knew had been there for a long time."

____

". . . Then, out of no where, the building shook and at one of the windows was a great white shark trying to get in! It would back away and hit the flimsy building again! I didn't know what to do except duck, and take refuge behind the old counter where the boy stood. He took an arrow from the pouch on his back, fitted it into his bow, aimed and it struck the shark right between the eyes, and it floated away, mortally wounded. . ."

____

"It was calm for the next several minutes," the man continued. "I think he realized my fear and he floated over and gave me a pat on the back. I knew my tank was running low, it only had enough air for about two hours and I had been submerged for well over an hour. I knew I had to get somewhere: fast!"

"With my finger, I pointed upwards: meaning I wanted to go up. He agreed with me and took me by the hand. But instead of going up he took me to a flat, shelter-like area, that was near the building where we were. The building had two doors, one opened, then you could enter. Only a small amount of water was allowed to come in. Then, that one closed and another 'inner', door opened, and an even smaller amount of water could come in. The inside of the area had air in it! It was like turning a glass upside down in dishwater: the air was trapped inside! I looked at the boy. I took off my tank and goggles. He took off his shell and goggles."

"This is a good area. Air is here. How did you know this was down here?" I asked looking around the room with amazement.

"I know all about this place. There are pockets of air all around this place. That is how we survive. It is a place I come to to rest when I am fishing," he said. *"You touched your back device: do you have air?"*

"Our air on our backs only holds about two hours," I told him.

"Good," he said. *"Then you have plenty of time for me to show you around our city. I think you will be intrigued."*

The reporter, Mr. Watkins, did not raise an eyebrow.

He continued to write.

"What happened then, Sir?" he asked, during a brief pause.

"We put on our gear: my tank and goggles. He put on his gear, his shell and goggles. He pointed to the door, he slid open the first one and we climbed in and he closed it behind us. Then he opened the outer door and the water rushed in, and the two of us floated outwards. He closed that door behind us. He took me on a tour: a tour of this strange city," he answered.

"A tour?" the reporter asked.

"Yes. We didn't go very far. He honored the fact that my air tank was low. But in a short time, I was able to see what once was obviously a great city, in ruins. I saw bars and hotels, and such, and yet, it appeared it had been hit by some great catastrophe. It was quite a brief trip," Mr. Hampton said.

"From what I could understand, Atlantis was a great city in it's time with a powerful Army that took over smaller, weaker cities in the region," the young reporter said.

Chapter

N*ine*

Mr. Hampton continued.

"It didn't look dominate; anything but that. It looked weak. The buildings that I saw were once made of morter, that was easy to see. And they were once sturdy. But that place had obviously been through something rough, the buildings had been down there for a long time and many of the buildings were cracked and molded, algie and seaweed had taken over the windows and doors. I could see schools of fish dwelling within them as I peeped inwards. It was not a pleasant sight to see. . . "

Mr. Hampton looked away.

"He finally took me by a place which was obviously a place of commerce, a city hall, if you will, that was once a place of legislature and decision making. But the statures that were there were broken, their heads missing, as were other body parts, their parts not even close to their origination. Something had shook them up. Again, it was a sad sight to see."

"This time the boy fingered me, and pointed to his right. I wondered what could be there."

"We kept swimming until we reached another tunnel-like area. He signaled me again and he entered the tunnel and I followed him into it. After ten or fifteen minutes we came out into a clearing."

The reporter stopped writing and from his sitting position he looked at Mr. Hampton.

"...A clearing? What kind of a clearing?" he asked.

"It was a huge cave, and it seemed to go on for miles! And it seemed to be long and straight, very straight, so much so, I couldn't see the end."

"...And?"

"And we were in a long narrow river, a river of sea water only about twenty feet or so wide! And only about six or eight feet deep. I could see to the bottom of this long, narrow river! It's waters were *that* clear. It seemed half man made, half natural. Again there were twenty foot waterfalls coming from the left side of the cavern. I pulled my goggles from over my eyes and let them rest atop of my head."

"Where is this? Where are we?" I could but ask the boy.

"This is my home," he said, rather proudly.

"He began to swim ahead of me. I swam several feet behind him. Before too long I began to see places of *dwellings;* house-like structures on the right side of the shallow lake, carved out of the sides of the cave! I was enthralled! But it didn't hold nothing to what I saw next. *People!* People were on the right side of the long narrow, shallow river. They were outside, fixing fences, working in their yards or working on their houses, just like anyone, around the cave-like structures that was hewed out of rock."

The young reporter stopped writing and looked at Mr. Hampton.

"People? Five thousand feet below the surface of the ocean," he said, more of a statement than a question.

"Yes. I couldn't believe it myself! They were very friendly. They waved at Jeremy, the young aquaboy, my guide and some even called him by name. He waved back. He even came to the edge and offered them fish he had had on the side of his belt. They came to the edge of the narrow river and accepted them. We continued to swim onwards."

Mr. Hampton looked thoughtful. "Then we reached a certain house, or rather, a cave: it was a very large one. We climbed from the water. Jeremy, the boy, took off his fins; took off his tank and his goggles. He layed them aside."

"This is where I live," he said. *"Please, come in."*

"I took off my tank, it was very heavy out of the water. Then I took off my goggles and layed them on the ground as well. I followed the boy into a house that had an open area for a door, yet the door was missing. We walked in. A man greeted us. He came from the other side of the house. He seemed to come out of nowhere."

"A man?" the young reporter asked.

"Yes. It was the boys father."

"I see," Mr. Watkins, the reporter said. Then he asked: "What happened then?"

"He was ruler of the underwater sea world," said Mr. Hampton. "I should have figured it because of his nice dwellings and large house. He came out with his hands extended."

Jeremy, the boy, introduced us.

"Father, this is Julies Hampton, from the surface. Julies, this is my father, Samati, ruler of this nation," the boy said.

"I shook hands with the man but didn't realize the boy came from such illustriousness," Mr. Hampton said.

Jeremy, the boy, continued.

"We haven't seen one of them for hundreds of yeas, have we father?" he asked.

"Well now, welcome," the man said as he shook my hand.

"The man was a rather short, stocky man, oddly dressed in what appeared to be a robe, but so were the others I had seen along the river. I suppose to them *I* was the one in a wet suit and tank that seemed odd," Mr. Hampton said to the reporter. "I continued greeting the man."

"Yes. I lost my way," I told him. *"Your son has been most cordial and friendly. I am from America."*

"America?" the man asked thoughtfully.

"Don't worry," I said. *"You don't know where it is. But I know the history of this place. When it sank with your ancestors below the sea in an earthquake, America wasn't even a country yet."*

"And it is now?" the man asked.

"Very much so. About five thousand feet above the ocean floor and if you follow the sunset, one thousand five hundred miles," I told him, but graciously.

"He extended his hands to the floor. I noticed they sat on the floor instead of using chairs."

The man looked to the other end of the house.

"Mira! Bring us cool drinks!" he yelled.

"From in the back emerged a young girl. She had very dark features and appeared almost Black. My eyes lit up at her attractiveness, and she bowed graciously as she entered the room."

"Yes, Father?" she asked.

"We have a guest. Bring us water," he said.

Mr. Hampton looked at the young reporter.

"I thought it was odd to be surrounded by so much water, water was being served in the cave-like dwelling. Nonetheless, she arrived several moments later with four glasses on a tray and each of us took a glass."

She took a glass but started to leave.

The man, the ruler, Samati, stopped her. *"Please, my child, Join us."*

"The young girl sat in the mist of us and Samati introduced her. I was glad he did."

"This is my daughter, Mira, and Jeremy's sister. Mira, this is Mr. Julies Hampton, from someplace called America. A place, I am sure, no one has ever heard of."

"Say, hello to the man," Mira," **Jeremy said.**

"The girl nodded pleasantly at me," Mr. Hampton said.

"Hello," **she said.**

"We all turned our glasses upwards and drank. Then we put the glasses aside. The man, Samati, looked at me."

"So what brought you here, my friend?" **the man, Samati asked.**

"I was on a military expedition, diving below the sea, and as I said, I must have lost my way," **I told him.**

"It must be big at the top. I could see how that could happen, since our ancestors were forced here," **he agreed.**

"It seems bigger down here. How did all this happen? You people must have resillence beyond believe to have survived down here." **I said.**

"Don't say 'you people'; you are among us now, you are one of us, Mr. Hampton," **Samati, the ruler, said.**

"Yes," **I said to him in agreement.** *"But how do you manage?"*

"We manage. Fish are all in the sea. There is much eatable sea weed that grows wild for vegetation if one knows where to look. We have adapted. We have managed. The men here knows where to look, where to fish, to feed their families," **the man said.**

"How is all this possible: this oasis under the waters?" **I asked him.**

"The air is trapped inside these caves. And the fresh water from the waterfalls herein brings us fresh air and water from the surface to the insides of these caves. It is a cycle, and one that keeps this process going," **the man said.**

"Needless to say, I was mesmerized! I stood up and looked out of one of the open windows, there was no paynes, and I stared across the narrow river to the other side. There were no caves like the ones on the side they were on: the house sides. Instead I saw medium sized waterfalls coming in from holes in the sides of the caves that emptied

into very tall barrels, high off of the ground, a reservoir, that held fresh water. A very clever cycle."

I turned and looked at the man and his son, and his daughter.

"No wonder no one has ever heard of you! You don't need us to hear of you!" I yelled back to him.

Mr. Hampton looked at the reporter again.

"I came back and sat among them again. I looked at their

ruler."

"How many are here?"

"Four, maybe five thousand."

"Impressive," I said.

"The young girl looked at me."

"Would you like more water?" she asked, nicely.

"Yes, I would," I answered just as nicely.

"She stood up went away and returned with more water and handed it to me and I drank it. It was very refreshing."

"I noticed how the girl was looking at me. I think she was fascinated," Mr. Hampton said.

"I looked at the man."

"It is very nice here," I told him.

"It is good to have strangers say such things. How long will you be staying?" the man asked, almost immediately.

"Not long. In fact, I must go. My people: my own people, they'll be looking for me," I said.

"Then thank you for coming. You must do what you have to do. But before you go, the ocean is big. Fascinating. Please stay. We know how you came in: through the giant rock that fell from the surface. The cave with the two waterfalls: Please stay a while. Have some fun with us. Enjoy what we have to offer!" he said.

The girl stood up.

"We will go back to the giant waterfalls!" she said.

"Please," the man said.

"I hesitated, of course, I knew I had to get back. But ultimately I agreed and said: *'Okay. What harm can it do?'*"

"**W**e walked outside and got my gear, my tank and goggles. I knew from my guage that I had at least an hours worth of air. Jeremy got his goggles, fins and put on his sea shell on his back. The young girl emered from the house with goggles, fins and sea shell. They jumped into the shallow, narrow river and headed back to where we had come, towards the tunnel. Samati came from the house and I shook hands with him. Then I jumped into the river and followed them, waving back at the friendly man, Samiti, who had accepted me. Then I waved at the people along the rivers edge as we headed back."

"**W**e, the aqua-boy Jeremy and the girl saw a waterfall near the end of the narrow river. We climbed from the shallow river, got under the small falls and let the water flow over us. We screamed at the freshness of the soothing water. But soon it was time to go. We dove back into the narrow river, ducked below and soon we were in the tunnel. When we emerged, in the far distance we saw the buildings that were the sunken Atlantis and went over them. Soon we had gone over them and were back to the first tunnel. Afterwards we were back at the original cavern section with the two larger waterfalls. We got under the water again and let it flow over us as the waterfalls did before. After a short time we exited the cave and saw the large rock that he had seen as he came in, the rock that he knew finally that was only a fragment piece of the puzzle that had fallen from a great city."

"Then it was time to go. I shook their hands and upwards I went, waving back to the friends I had made. They waved back. I kept ascending. I knew my air supply was limited but adreneline kept me going. Then my air supply became limited. But then, I could see the top, the very surface of the waters! I reached for the top before my air supply became dry!"

"And then my head was on top of the waters!"

Chapter

T*en*

The reporter had started writing again with his pad and pen. He looked at Mr. Hampton, his eyes full of wonder but, but continuing to listen to the old man's story.

"So you were out in the middle of the ocean: then what, Sir?" he asked.

12 hours after dive

"**I** didn't know what I would do. There I was out in the middle of the open sea. I looked below me. And as I looked to my right and to my left, I saw nothing. I knew, however, that the problem was to avoid freezing, or sinking out in the open waters. And avoiding sharks! I loosened my heavy air tank, it was empty anyway, and I let it go. It plummet to the deep. But at least I was able to swim. But that was all I was able to do for hours. My wet suit

helped. But it's effect didn't last long. Then night came. I began to

wrinkle up, my hands was wrinkling, all of me: I began to freeze in

the cold choppy waters and the frigidness was almost unbearable. I

thought there was no way out!"

"Then I heard a long sound, like a horn, and then a light that went back and forth. It was a search light and they were looking for me! I held my hands high. I yelled to the top of my voice!:

"HERE I AM!" I screamed.

"I waved. Each time I waved, I went under a bit more. But as I was waving and going under for the third time, they spotted me, lowered a boat and two men came out and got me. They pulled me in."

". . .You were rescued," the young reporter said.

"Yes. But the problem only started there. They wondered where I was all that time and how I was able to be out there all alone for nearly a day when two men couldn't; only Timmings, the man you interviewed, being found ten hours before they pulled me in," Mr. Hampton said. "They wondered where I was?"

"And what did you tell them?" the young reporter asked.

"What could I tell them? I told them the truth. That I was out there among some people below the ocean that offered me water until I could get back here," I said.

"You didn't," the reporter said.

"I did."

"What did they say?"

"They looked at me like I was some kind of a nut. The offered me the care of a good phychiatrist. I refused. I thought I was in big trouble. But they said I had done a good thing. But at last, I was discharged with honors. I guess in my 'heroism' they overlooked anything else," Mr. Hampton said.

"What do you feel, deep inside? Do you think it was real, Sir? Those people?" the young reporter asked.

"Yep."

"Is that the end of it then? You're going to let them just push this under the rug?" the reporter asked.

"Well, yes and no. You see, they sent another ship out there with this sonar capabilities. And they spotted this huge rock, and the sound bounced off of it just about where I was. They let me go out there just to stir them in the right direction: the right area. Well, they sent back for another ship with Navy frogmen in full gear, and they dove nearly a mile down to this rock and examined it inside and out. And what do you think they said? They examined that thing and the area around it an said: 'although it looked man made, the formation in question was obviously of nature, and no man had anything to do with it, and no men had the capabilities before us to go this far down; even though there seemed to be 'steps' involved."

"You're kidding? Was that the final analysis?" the young reporter asked.

"Nope. If they would have gone fifty yards to the right of that, they would have found the tunnel: the tunnel where the first waterfalls were. The tunnel that would have led them to the cave. But they didn't. And they were just a few feet from one of the most fantastic discoveries of this century."

The young reporter looked away. Mr. Hampton looked away. He looked about here and there.

"Nice day isn't it today, isn't it Sonny?"

The reporter looked in the same directions.

"Yes Sir, Mr. Hampton," he said.

The reporter paused.

He stood up. He took his notes, tore them up into itty bitty pieces and let them fall uselessly in all directions to the ground. "I won't tell if you won't."

"Not in the least, Sonny," Mr. Hampton said.

The young reporter looked at Mr. Hampton.

"Like you say, Sir, it's a beautiful day."

"Beautiful."

"It's getting late, though. Dinner?"

"Sounds good," Mr. Hampton said.

The reporter went to the back of the wheelchair and started to push Mr. Hampton towards the upwards wheelchair friendly ramp.

--THE END -

Dear Reader,

Thank you for reading 'Tour of Atlantis'. Won't you please consider posting a short, brief, polite review? Honest reader reviews help others decide if they would enjoy a book. Again, thanks for the read and have a nice day!!

Sincerely,

-the author-

-Walt Foster has always been a fan of mysteries and science fiction and he loves to write them. He lives in the United States U.S.A.

Don't miss out!

Visit the website below and you can sign up to receive emails whenever Walter Foster publishes a new book. There's no charge and no obligation.

https://books2read.com/r/B-A-BRFW-WGHEC

Connecting independent readers to independent writers.

Did you love *Tour of Atlantis*? Then you should read *Blackula the Vampire!*[1] by Walter Foster!

[2]

Ann Thomas is an attractive lawyer and an African American woman. She has inherited a remote farm outside of Atlanta once owned by her grandmother, a former slave.

Unknowingly to her, her grandmother was once in a romantic relationship with a well-to-do African man back in the year 1890. But the romance went sour when Ann's grandmother decided to marry someone else. Things were quiet, and through the years the jilted African man had not forgotten Ann's grandmother.

Nearly two hundred years later and in current times, he sees Ann's picture in a newspaper outlining *'outstanding lawyers'* and he confuses Ann with her grandmother!

---

1. https://books2read.com/u/bOnQPJ

2. https://books2read.com/u/bOnQPJ

Suddenly, he wants her back and he is coming after her, two hundred years later with determination to win her again, and this time he would let nothing stand in his way!

Also by Walter Foster

Tour of Atlantis
The House on the Edge of Homerville
Blackula the Vampire!
The Invisible Man
Blackenstein
Diamonds on Mars!
Fragments: Abort Martian Landing
Madam Black Soothsayer - Fortune Teller

About the Author

Walt Foster has always been a fan of mysteries and science fiction and he loves to write them. He is a graduate of Central Carolina Technical College in South Carolina. He lives in the United States U.S.A.

About the Publisher

The New Star Press - U.S.A.